Holding Steady: Leadership reflections from Days of Uncertainty

Dr. Sami Mohammed Handley, DBA, MA, FCIPD

Disclaimer

This book is a work of reflective non-fiction. It records personal observations, emotions, and leadership reflections during a period of regional uncertainty. It is not intended as factual reporting, political analysis, operational commentary, or an official account of events.

Any references to public atmosphere, changes in daily routines, leadership responses, family dynamics, or workplace experiences are presented as lived experience and interpretation. The intention of this book is human and developmental: to explore how individuals, families, and leaders hold steady when certainty becomes fragile.

All names, identifying details, and situational specifics have been limited or generalized where appropriate.

Dedication

To the people who continued.

To those who woke each morning and carried on with the quiet routines of daily life, even while uncertainty lingered beyond the horizon.

To the families who checked on one another, the colleagues who offered reassurance, and the communities that chose calm when anxiety might have been easier.

History often remembers the dramatic moments of conflict, the headlines and the turning points that shape the course of events. Yet what sustains societies is rarely dramatic. It is the steady character of ordinary people.

It is the quiet resilience that keeps cities moving, workplaces functioning, and communities connected even during uncertain times.

The words of wisdom from our leaders, 'we are no easy target, we have thick skin but bitter flesh,' resonated across the region, making everyone feel as one.

These pages are dedicated to those individuals, the many who chose steadiness, patience, and calm while the world around them seemed less certain.

Prologue: The quiet before

Before uncertainty arrived, life moved with reassuring predictability. Across the United Arab Emirates, cities followed rhythms that had become second nature, patterns repeated so consistently that they seemed permanent. Morning light spread across skylines of glass and steel, reflecting from towers that had come to symbolize progress, ambition, and order. Roads filled steadily with traffic as commuters moved toward offices, schools, shops, and construction sites, each journey part of a larger routine that connected millions of individual lives. Buildings came to life floor by floor, office lights turning on, elevators moving, reception desks opening, and the quiet machinery of another working day beginning with practiced efficiency.

Children went to school with bags packed and schedules already known. Parents organized mornings around drop-offs, meetings, errands, and obligations that had long since become habit. Conversations centered on work, family, and future plans. People spoke of promotions, school terms, business growth, travel arrangements, investments, and the next steps of ordinary life. Stability was not something people discussed often, because it did not feel fragile enough to require discussion. It was simply assumed, woven so deeply into daily experience that it seemed less like a condition and more like a fact.

Days unfolded with a kind of unspoken agreement, as though the world itself had settled into a dependable routine. Time moved according to calendars, appointments, school runs, lunch breaks, and evening plans. There was comfort in repetition. The familiar sequence of each day gave people a sense of direction, even when life was busy or demanding. One day resembled the next closely enough to create confidence that tomorrow would arrive in much the same form as today.

The hum of air conditioning blended with the distant sounds of construction and passing cars, forming a backdrop so constant it was barely noticed. It was the sound of modern life continuing without interruption. Cranes moved in the distance, roads carried a steady flow of vehicles, and doors opened and closed in offices, malls, and apartment towers. Elevators rose and descended, phones rang, deliveries arrived, and schedules were kept. These small, ordinary sounds rarely drew attention precisely because they were always there.

Cafés opened their doors to familiar faces, where baristas prepared the same orders without needing to ask. Morning customers arrived at nearly the same hour, taking the same seats, glancing at the same phones, greeting the same staff with the easy recognition that routine creates. Coffee cups were set down before names were spoken. Brief conversations repeated themselves in comforting variations, about traffic, meetings, weather, deadlines, or weekend plans.

Colleagues gathered over coffee, exchanging updates that felt comfortably repetitive. They spoke of projects in progress, upcoming targets, minor frustrations, and predictable workplace concerns. There was reassurance in those ordinary exchanges. Nothing dramatic needed to happen for life to feel full. The repetition itself carried value. It suggested continuity, and continuity suggested security.

Across neighborhoods and city centers alike, routines linked strangers who never spoke but moved through the same spaces each day. Security guards recognized residents by sight. Shopkeepers knew regular customers. Receptionists expected familiar arrivals. Teachers prepared classrooms. Drivers followed known routes. Families planned evenings around work hours, school schedules, and shared meals. The ordinary details of life created a wider sense of steadiness that stretched beyond any one household.

Even ambition existed within structure. People planned ahead because the future felt reachable and organized. Goals could be mapped. Savings could be built. Careers could progress step by step. The pace of life was active, often demanding, but it remained legible. People knew where they were within the rhythm of things.

That was the nature of the time before uncertainty arrived. Life did not feel dramatic, but it felt dependable. And because it felt dependable, many hardly noticed how much comfort that certainty provided until it was no longer there.

Evenings carried their own gentle rhythm. Families returned home at predictable hours, streets softened under the glow of streetlights, and the pace of the day eased into quiet domesticity. Dinner tables became spaces of routine conversation, small stories from school, workplace anecdotes, plans for the weekend, each detail reinforcing a sense of continuity. Weekends, too, followed patterns: visits to malls, walks along the waterfront, gatherings with friends that required little planning because they were already part of an unchanging cycle.

There was a quiet confidence woven into everyday life, a belief that tomorrow would resemble today, and the day after would follow suit. People made plans without hesitation, holidays months in advance, investments years into the future, because the ground beneath them felt steady. Change, when it came, was gradual and expected, something that could be anticipated and managed.

In this landscape of certainty, time seemed to move forward without disruption, each moment linking seamlessly to the next. It was not a life of grand revelations or constant excitement, but of something subtler and, in many ways, more comforting: the assurance that things would continue as they always had.

The region itself had never been without complexity. Political tensions, shifting alliances, and competing interests had long existed in the background of global affairs. Yet for most people, these forces remained distant, part of the wider world, not something that shaped the texture of daily life.

What makes moments of uncertainty so striking is not that tensions exist. It is how quickly they move from the background into the foreground, where stability rarely announces itself while it is present and yet becomes visible only when it begins to shift.

Looking back, there are always signs, conversations becoming more cautious, news coverage more frequent, speculation growing about what might come next. But in the moment, these signals are easy to overlook, life continues, routines hold and the assumption remains that tomorrow will look much like today.

Until, quietly, it doesn't.

These pages begin shortly after that shift.

Author's Note

This book did not begin with the intention of becoming a book; it began as a habit.

Like many others, I found myself living through a period where something in the atmosphere of daily life had shifted. Events beyond our immediate control were unfolding quickly, bringing with them a quiet but persistent sense of uncertainty.

In times like these, there is never a shortage of analysis, commentary, or opinion. What felt less visible to me, however, was something far simpler, an honest account of what it feels like to live through such days, as a father, a son and a leaders, one day at a time.

I had experienced periods of disruption before. Growing up in the United Kingdom, I lived through moments shaped by the Northern Ireland conflict, the Thatcher era, and the collapse of industries that affected entire communities, but I never recorded those experiences. I never paused to capture what they felt like in the moment; this time, I did.

Each evening, I began writing, not with a plan, and not with an audience in mind, but as a way to make sense of what I was observing around me. It started quietly, almost without intention. A notebook opened at the end of the day, a pen moving across the page not out of discipline, but out of a need to gather thoughts that refused to settle on their own.

I found myself drawn to the small moments, the kind that might have once gone unnoticed. A pause in someone's voice during an otherwise ordinary conversation. The way people lingered a little longer on certain topics, as if searching for reassurance that wasn't quite there. Glances exchanged without words, carrying more weight than anything spoken aloud. These fragments of everyday life began to feel significant, as though they were part of something forming just beneath the surface.

Conversations, too, began to shift in subtle ways. Familiar discussions about work or routine carried an undercurrent that hadn't been there before. There were hesitations where there had once been ease, careful phrasing where words had once come freely. People still spoke of plans and expectations, but there was a slight distance in how they did so, as if those plans no longer felt entirely within their control.

These pages were written in real time, without the benefit of hindsight and without any intention to interpret political decisions or global developments. History will inevitably document those.

What interested me was something else entirely: how people respond when stability is no longer guaranteed. How routine becomes an anchor, how resilience, character, how leaders perform in times that cannot be planned, how they display resilience and the calm that is reveale in the most ordinary moments.

If this book serves any purpose beyond personal reflection, it is perhaps this:

To offer a record of leadership resilience, a record of how life continues during uncertain times and how, in the absence of clear answers, people often rely on something far more fundamental, which is steadiness, not loud or dramatic, but consistent, grounded and human.

These reflections are simply that, a record of days as they were experienced, while the future was still unknown.

Table of Contents

Prequel: The days before it started

Conflicts rarely begin on the day the world first notices them.

By the time headlines appear, statements are issued, and questions are asked, the conditions that led to those moments have often been forming quietly for some time. What seems sudden to the public is often the visible outcome of pressures that developed gradually, out of sight and without immediate recognition. The period leading up to these events was no different.

Across the region, pressures had been steadily building. Geopolitical tensions, shifting alliances, economic interests, and long-standing regional dynamics were all evolving beneath the surface. None of these forces operated in isolation. Each influenced the others, creating a climate in which uncertainty did not arrive all at once, but accumulated over time.

Relationships between states were being reassessed. Strategic priorities were changing. Economic considerations remained deeply connected to political decisions, while older rivalries and unresolved disputes continued to shape the atmosphere in ways that were not always visible to ordinary observers. Long-established balances required constant maintenance, and even small shifts carried wider implications.

No single factor explains what followed. It was not the result of one event or one disagreement alone. Rather, it emerged from multiple pressures moving in the same direction, reinforcing one another until the broader environment became more fragile than it appeared.

Yet for most people, this remained largely unseen.

News updates came and went, as they often do. Political statements were made. Officials spoke in careful language. Analysts debated possible outcomes, offering competing interpretations of what developments might mean. Some warnings were raised, some concerns dismissed, and much of it blended into the constant flow of international news that people had learned to observe without feeling personally affected.

For many, these developments seemed distant from everyday life.

Workplaces remained busy. Meetings were held. Emails were answered. Shops opened on time. Roads stayed full. Schools continued their schedules. Plans were made for the week ahead, then the month ahead, then beyond. The ordinary pace of life has a way of creating the impression that larger forces are happening somewhere else, affecting other people in other places.

Cities moved at their usual rhythm. Offices operated with familiar efficiency. Families focused on responsibilities, routines, and future plans. Conversations about global events often remained secondary to the immediate concerns of daily living , deadlines, bills, appointments, children, health, and the practical demands of ordinary life.

Even when regional developments were discussed, they were often treated as background noise rather than approaching reality. Headlines might be noticed in the morning and forgotten by the afternoon. Commentary was consumed briefly, then replaced by the next task, the next obligation, the next routine concern.

This is often how uncertainty gathers.
Not with dramatic interruption at first, but in the background of normal life. Signals appear gradually. Tensions rise incrementally. Public attention moves elsewhere. What is developing remains partially obscured by the continuity of everyday routines.
That was the atmosphere in the days before it started.

Life still appeared stable. Systems still functioned. The visible world still moved as expected. Yet beneath that surface, pressures were aligning in ways that would soon become impossible to ignore. I question how leaders work with such pressures, how they display presence with resilence, thoughtfulness and humility. Often as a leader, such events can break the strongest, but yet what has surface so far is greatness, steadfastness and without doubt strength of conviction to protect was holding firm.

There were moments, of course, brief conversations, passing questions, like:

What if this really happens?
Would anyone actually follow through?

But these thoughts rarely lingered; yes, they were acknowledged, then set aside, as routine took over once again, and what makes periods like this so significant is the contrast that follows. One day, events feel remote, something observed from a distance. Next, they feel closer, more immediate, even if daily life has not yet visibly changed. The shift itself is rarely dramatic; it is gradual, subtle, and almost unnoticeable at first.

A growing awareness, a change in tone, a sense that the wider environment is becoming less certain. It was within that space, between normality and realization that these reflections began, not as commentary on political decisions or international affairs, but as observations of something more immediate:

How people experience uncertainty when it begins to touch everyday life

The First Night

There is often a moment when distant events begin to feel closer.

Until that moment arrives, conflict can seem contained within headlines, maps, official statements, and the language of analysts. It belongs to the wider world, something serious perhaps, but still removed from the immediate texture of daily life. People observe it from a distance, aware of it but not yet touched by it. Then something changes, and what once felt far away begins to move inward.

For many people, that moment arrived late in the evening.

News updates had been circulating throughout the day. Reports of unusual activities across the region appeared in steady succession. Statemenst were being issued. Analysts speculated about possible responses, wider implications, and whether events would escalate or stabilize. The language of uncertainty-filled broadcasts and digital feeds, yet for most people, these developments still felt remote.

They belonged to the category of events people follow without believing they will directly shape the next hour of their own lives.

Daily routines had continued. Work had ended for many. Families were at home. Meals had been shared. Some were preparing for the next day, others unwinding after the demands of the current one. Screens carried updates in the background, but ordinary life still held its familiar shape. Concern existed, but it remained abstract.

Then the atmosphere shifted.

It did not happen through a single announcement so much as through a sudden change in tone and tempo. Phones began to light up with alerts. Messages circulated quickly between friends, family members, and colleagues. Questions replaced commentary. People began checking multiple sources at once. What earlier seemed like distant reporting now carried a different urgency.

Television coverage changed tone as reports emerged of never seen before activities across the Gulf.

Presenters who had spoken with measured detachment now sounded more immediate. Graphics appeared. Live updates replaced broader discussion. Breaking news banners remained on screen. Commentary narrowed from speculation to active developments. Viewers who had only half been paying attention now focused fully.

The shift was not only informational. It was emotional.

Something in the room changes when distant events feel nearer than before. Conversations become shorter and more direct, routine pauses. Background noise becomes foreground concern. People look again at messages, refresh news feeds, and listen more carefully than they did an hour earlier.

The ordinary evening rhythm gave way to heightened attention.

Friends checked on one another. Colleagues exchanged updates. Families asked practical questions. Some searched for confirmation. Others tried to remain calm. Information moved quickly, but certainty did not move with it. Reports arrived faster than understanding.

For many, that was the first real sense that events elsewhere might not remain elsewhere.

The language of the day had been diplomatic statements, military reports, and expert analysis. The language of the night became alerts, messages, and immediate reaction. The distance between observer and participant, while still incomplete, had begun to narrow.

That is how such moments often begin.

Not always with what is seen directly, but with the realization that the boundary between world events and personal life has become thinner than it seemed only hours earlier.

And on that first night, many felt that change at once.

Some people stepped outside onto balconies or into quiet streets, looking toward the sky, unsure, but yet inquisitive about what they might see or hear. Others stayed indoors, watching the news, refreshing updates, or calling family members to check whether they had heard the same reports.

In cities, towns and small villages that are normally defined by movement and light, there was a brief moment of stillness; it wasn't panic, more like awareness.

It was the recognition that something unfolding far beyond the horizon had suddenly become part of the shared experience of the region. For many people, daily life would continue the following morning much as it always had. Offices would open, schools would operate, traffic would return to its familiar rhythm.

Yet something subtle had changed.

Nothing outwardly dramatic needed to happen for that change to be felt. Streets still functioned, businesses still opened, routines still continued, and daily obligations still demanded attention. On the surface, much of life appeared unchanged. But beneath that surface, awareness had shifted. The sense of distance that once separated ordinary life from regional events had weakened.

From that night onward, people were paying closer attention to the news.

Updates that might previously have been glanced at briefly were now followed more carefully. Headlines were read in full. Notifications were checked more often. Broadcasts remained on longer. Information that had once felt peripheral now carried a different weight. People wanted not only to know what had happened, but what might happen next.

They were also paying closer attention to anecdotes describing experiences.

Personal accounts began to matter in a new way. Stories from friends, relatives, colleagues, and acquaintances were listened to more closely than before. What someone had seen, heard, felt, or noticed became part of how others understood the moment. Individual experiences, however small, carried significance because they offered texture beyond official statements and headlines.

Conversations around the situation became the norm.

What had previously been an occasional discussion became a regular topic. In workplaces, homes, cafés, and messages between friends, people returned to the same questions repeatedly. They compared information, shared interpretations, repeated what they had heard, and tried to make sense of developments that were still unfolding. Some spoke with confidence, others with caution, but nearly everyone was paying attention in some form.

There was also a growing awareness that the days ahead might carry a different atmosphere than the days before.

This awareness was not always dramatic or openly expressed. Often it existed quietly, in the background of thought. Plans were still made, routines still followed, responsibilities still met. Yet alongside these normal patterns was a new sense that ordinary life might no longer feel quite as settled as it once had. The future, even in the short term, seemed less certain than it had only days earlier.

It was during this period of heightened awareness that the reflections contained in this diary began.

They did not begin as an attempt to document military events, strategic developments, or the conflict itself. Others would report those matters through headlines, statements, and analysis. These pages began for a different reason.

They began as a record of atmosphere, a record of how how leaders would show strength and resilience.

A record of how people quietly lived through uncertainty while continuing with ordinary life. A record of moods, conversations, routines, adjustments, and the subtle emotional changes that accompany larger events. A record of what it feels like when history moves nearby, even if daily life outwardly continues.

Not as a record of the conflict itself, but as a record of how people quietly lived through it.

Introduction

There is a particular kind of quiet that appears when the world becomes uncertain.
Cities continue to move, people go to work, conversations take place, life appears, outwardly, unchanged. Yet beneath the surface, there is a different awareness, an unspoken understanding that something larger is unfolding.

It is in these moments that people reveal more about themselves than they often realize.
Some search for answers, some believe they have them, others look for reassurance, but most simply try to hold on to the familiar rhythm of everyday life.

I began writing these pages during such days, not because the events themselves required another record; history will capture the timelines, the headlines, and the decisions that shaped them.
What interested me far more was something quieter and often overlooked: how people think, behave, and lead when certainty disappears.
In uncertain times, character reveals itself in small moments, a conversation, a gesture, a pause where calm is chosen over reaction.

This diary was not written with hindsight; it was written day by day, in real time, without knowing what would come next.
It is not an analysis of events, nor an attempt to explain them.
It is simply a reflection of what it felt like to live through them, to continue working, leading, and living, while the world around you quietly shifted, because in the end, what sustains people during uncertain times is not always clarity.

It is steadiness.

Day 1 – First Diary Entry 28th February 2026

"The sound that didn't belong"

I woke earlier than usual today, not by choice, but pulled from sleep by a sound that didn't belong. It wasn't loud in the way that demands immediate panic, but it carried enough weight to interrupt the stillness of the morning. A dull, distant unusual noise, far enough to feel removed, yet close enough that it couldn't be dismissed as nothing. For a moment, I lay still, suspended between sleep and awareness, listening carefully, as if the silence that followed might explain what I had just heard.

Then came the jets.

They moved fast, too fast to be mistaken for anything routine. Their sound cut sharply through the morning sky, deliberate and focused, lacking the familiar, almost forgettable hum of commercial flights that usually passed overhead. There was a precision to it, a sense of urgency that felt out of place against the calm that typically defined early hours in our city

I stayed where I was, listening more intently now, trying to place the pattern. Normally, by this time, there would already be a steady rhythm above, planes descending in intervals, engines blending into a continuous backdrop of motion. It was a sound so constant it often went unnoticed, something you only recognised in its absence.

And that was what stood out the most.

There were no commercial aircraft. No distant layering of engines. No gradual rise and fall of sound that marked the routine movement of air traffic. Just an open, unsettled silence, interrupted only by the sharp, passing streaks of jets overhead. The contrast was immediate and unmistakable. Something had shifted, and the sky, usually so active, felt abruptly empty.

I reached for my phone, the motion almost instinctive, as if confirmation was already expected. The screen lit up, and within seconds, the fragments of information had begun to take shape. Notifications, headlines, partial updates, all forming a single, coherent message that left little room for interpretation:

"Our airspace had been temporarily closed for safety reasons"

That line stayed with me longer than I expected.

The drive to work felt unusually still, roads open, movement without momentum, as though the city was operating half a step behind itself. Inside, everything appeared normal.

People at their desks, screens on, meetings beginning, yet beneath it all, there was a shared awareness, subtle but unmistakable, something had definitely shifted. No one fully said it, but everyone seemed to feel it. What I noticed most was not fear; it was attentiveness, people listening more closely, reading more carefully, thinking just a little further ahead than usual.

Moments like this have a way of revealing just how much of life rests on a kind of stability we rarely stop to examine. It exists in the background, unspoken and unquestioned, shaping our expectations without ever needing to be acknowledged. We move through our days with the quiet assumption that things will continue as they have been, that tomorrow will unfold much like today, following patterns we have come to trust without thinking.

It is only when that assumption is gently, almost imperceptibly disrupted that its presence becomes clear. The shift does not have to be dramatic. Even a slight fracture in that sense of continuity is enough to alter the way everything is perceived. Familiar surroundings begin to feel different, not because they have visibly changed, but because the certainty attached to them has begun to loosen.

In that space, awareness sharpens. Ordinary details take on a new weight, and the act of observing becomes more deliberate. Things that once blended into routine begin to stand out, not as anomalies, but as reminders of how much we rely on the expectation of sameness. The world itself remains intact, yet it is experienced differently, filtered through the subtle understanding that what once felt guaranteed may no longer be as certain as it seemed.

At work, I realized early that today was not about answers; it was about presence. Not over-speaking, not speculating, just creating enough steadiness for people to continue doing what they do best, showing up, because when uncertainty first arrives, people don't immediately look for solutions. They look for signals, calm or concern, clarity or confusion, direction or hesitation, and whether we realize it or not, those signals often come from us.

The remarkable thing about societies is their instinct for continuity. Even in moments like this, people return to routine, work continues, conversations continue, life continues.

Perhaps this is where resilience begins, not in reaction, but in repetition.

At home, it felt distant; at work, the crisis was discussed, but cautiously; no one quite knew what it meant yet. The world hadn't taken a position.

What today taught me:

When certainty fades, people instinctively look for steadiness.

This where I say, leadership begins the moment certainty ends, not with answers, but with presence.

Day 2 – 1st March: *The echo of it*

The morning came with the same sounds, but they landed differently today, less surprising and more expected, but I questioned myself, should I be thinking like this so early into the conflict? After all, it wasn't ours, meaning this war didn't belong in the here. But that's how quickly the mind adjusts; what unsettled you yesterday starts to feel like part of the pattern today.

I noticed people checking their phones more, not openly, just subtle glances. News apps started to refresh more. Messages, phone calls coming in from family, friends, from different parts of the region and the world.

But for me, there's still no clear narrative as to why and the what, just fragments, updates without resolution, but still with a mindset that this would be here for a few days and then it would be over.

At work, conversations have shifted. Less about work, more about context.

"Did you hear it?"
"Where was it?"
"What are they saying now?"
"What news channels are you using?"

No one is panicking. But no one is relaxed either, but you could sense that there's a quiet tension, like everyone is holding a thought, an inner feeling, maybe a disconnection they haven't fully voiced yet. What I realized today is that in the absence of clarity, people fill the gaps themselves.

So, I spoke, not with certainty, but with honesty. I was learning rapidly that every single person was dealing with this very differently, but I had to make the call, albeit some would call it blunt or emotionless, but this was not the time to derail our emotions, humility as a leader in such situations is crucial for everyones wellbeing, its our duty to filter and create clarity.

Here's what we know.
Here's what we don't.

Here's what we're doing.

However, what brought the initial days into reality were these statistics of what had been happening, a clear reality that this wasn't just a 1 day playground fight.

Information like this requires the leaders to removing the space where fear can grow. Whoever we lead or love, we need to keep the clarity, facts help, no embroidery, no assumptions needed.

If theres one statement I would make it is, people don' t need noise in uncertainty , they need clarity they can hold onto

Day 3 – 2nd March: The weight of awareness

Where I live, theres a daily routine to watch the usual commercial flights overhead, you could almost set the time of day with the regular frequency of flights, but today the sky looks different now.
You wouldn't notice it immediately, but once you do, you can't ignore it. Fewer aircraft, less noise, maybe it was more like a controlled movement, less randomness perhaps!

Inside, I can feel something building, not fear, I personally don't phase easily, but awareness was building, let us call it a constant low-level alertness that doesn't switch off.

But definitely you start listening more closely to sounds, sometimes these sounds are in your head, or sometimes when a door bangs or a football hits a gate, the new awareness makes you think very differently. You check updates without thinking, purposeful and becoming almost habitual, you read headlines twice, and still revisit to make sure you haven't misread. That kind of awareness is tiring, quietly but steadily tiring.

At work, productivity is still there, but it's layered with distraction; heads that were normally down working on priorities became updated with news. Yes, people are present, but part of their attention is elsewhere.

I made a conscious decision today to slow things down, not the work, but the way we move through it, more check-ins with the team and colleagues, more pauses, more space for people to just speak.
You might ask why, but it's because what I'm starting to understand is this:
You don't manage performance in moments like this; you manage people.

Key headlines were highlighting that there were airspace changes. Travel advisory statements, quiet adjustments that signaled awareness without alarm and official statements remained balanced deliberately.

As a leader, you don' t manage performance in uncertainty, you manage people

Day 4 – 3rd March: When it enters the room

Today, it stopped being distant; the stories came in, not from the news, but from people who were clearly shaken or disturbed, especially those living in other parts of the Country

Stories started to emerge with real experiences which brought a degree of reality into the room, examples such as windows shaking in the early hours, a faint smell through air vents, and children waking up confused by the noise.

There was nothing catastrophic, but enough to unhinge people, enough to move this from something "out there" to something that has crossed into homes, into personal space, into reality, and for me, I could feel the shift instantly, voices slightly lower, conversations slightly heavier with political insights and fragments of views and assumptions.

At work, I found myself being more visible today, walking the floor more than usual. Sitting in spaces I wouldn't normally sit, not to lead, but to be present, because in moments like this, people don't need instructions, they need to see that someone is steady, someone who has routine and structure and most definitely someone who isn't fazed easily.

The real shift isn' t in events, it' s in how people feel them, connecting, visualizing, understanding each behavioral space has now become the daily norm as a leader.

Day 5 – 4th March: The slow build of fatigue

There's no headline today that changes everything, and yet, today felt the heaviest so far, maybe because there's a degree of insecurity as to when this will stop.

Five days of broken sleep.
Five days of constant updates.
Five days of not quite knowing.
It adds up, you see it in small ways, shorter responses, less patience, a slight edge where there normally isn't one.

I felt it myself today, that subtle shift in energy, it wasn't exhaustion, but a kind of emotional weight that sits just beneath the surface, and the only thing I could do was adjust, not change, but quietly adjust, less pressure on timelines, more understanding during conversations, empathy, but still displaying resilience.
What we learn, whether personal or work, pushing harder right now doesn't create results.
It creates cracks.

Day 6 – 5th March: *The adjustment*

Something changed today, not externally, but internally. Was it the fact that people are starting to adapt, or at the extreme, making contingency plans to go to their homeland? These realizations were surfacing at speed. It was the first time I heard families from abroad place a subtle pressure on loved ones to come home.

The sounds are still there. The uncertainty remains, but the reaction to it is softer, more measured. Routines are reforming, team check-ins are progressing, not perfectly, with a degree of lack of urgency, but still consistency prevailed. It's resilience, but not the loud kind, the quiet kind, the kind that shows up without announcement, that was my aim, keeping everyone's chin up, including my own. As a leader, I focused on reinforcing that today, acknowledging effort, noticing consistency, keeping things steady, but I am aware, very aware, that this phase can be misleading because just as people adapt, they can also become numb.

And that's a risk in itself, but as a leaders, I began to understand even more that resilience is not a reaction it is repetition under pressure.

Day 7 – 6th March: *The power of people*

Today, I saw something I hadn't seen all week: connection, people checking in on each other, offering support without being asked, small conversations that go beyond work.
There's a shared understanding forming, understanding each one's way of dealing with things, unspoken, but strong, and yes, the moment surfaced where I began to realize that we're all experiencing this in different ways, but we're in it together, and that matters.

But I also noticed the quieter ones, the ones who say "I'm fine" a little too quickly, the ones who stay focused, but slightly withdrawn, so I spent more time there today, because leadership isn't just about the visible energy in the room, it's about the energy that isn't being shown.

At home, things were changing; emotional dynamics in the house became more tense, worrying where this might end, contingency discussions, fears never heard or dreamt of before were now commonplace. The TV was playing in the background, but with no focus from those who watched, too busy watching news reels, listening to social media became an evening routine.

The numbness from day 6 has now become the norm both at work, in society and at home.

My lesson was to keep watching those around you to be their anchor, as they were becoming frail and in need of a calm voice.

Day 8 – 7th March: The questions no one can answer

The tone shifted again today; it's no longer just about what's happening, it's about what it means.

"How long will this go on?"
"What if it escalates?"
"What does this mean for us... Really?"

These are different questions now, heavier, longer-term, harder to hold, and the truth is I don't have the answers, that sat with me today, not comfortably, but honestly.
There's a natural instinct in leadership to fill that space, to provide direction, reassurance, something definitive, but today, I chose a different approach, I grounded people in what is certain, reminding everyone listening that we are here, we are operating, we are supporting each other, and within our own walls, we are safe, sometimes, that's enough.

But today brought something else, something I hadn't experienced before. I was in the garden when I noticed am unusual movement above, cutting across the sky toward the sea. Its path felt deliberate, focused, and for a moment, I wondered what it was, but I couldn't see clearly enough to understand. Then came the sound, loud, immediate, with no second guesses as to what it was.

For a second, everything stood still, not out of confusion but recognition, this wasn't distant anymore, this wasn't theoretical, this was real and that moment stayed with me, not as a scar but as something etched deeper, a reminder that what we had been discussing, analyzing, and trying to rationalize... was no longer abstract, it was visible, and once you see it, you carry it differently.

The conversations today reflected that shift, less speculation, more awareness, more weight behind every question.

As a leader, I felt the need to stay even more grounded, not to remove uncertainty but to absorb some of it, because when questions have no answers, what people look for is not certainty; they look for steadiness.

What today taught me:

When answers are unavailable, presence becomes the answer.

Day 9 – 8th March: Holding the Line

Determination is beginning to show itself now, not loudly, not in any dramatic way, but it's there. No one is pretending this is easy anymore; the conversations have moved beyond that. The initial curiosity, the questioning, even the underlying tension, all of it has settled into something more defined.
People are showing up, doing what needs to be done, continuing with their roles, holding their responsibilities without being asked.

From the outside, it could almost pass as normal, supermarkets busy with families buying for Iftar, but beneath it, I can sense something else, a sustained effort.
The kind that doesn't announce itself, but you can feel it in the room, in the way people pause slightly longer, in the way energy is managed more carefully, in the quiet moments and between conversations.
I tell myself that this is resilience, but not the kind that can run indefinitely without support, and that's where the focus needed to be today, not change, not a new direction, just consistency, same tone, same presence. no surprises.

Because in uncertain environments, people don't just look at what you say, they watch for what changes, and when nothing unnecessary shifts, it creates something powerful where consistency becomes stability, and over time, stability becomes trust, not declared, earned.

Today, the narrative widened; it wasn't just about strategy anymore. It was about impact on travel, on safety, on daily life; governments began addressing people more directly, and you certainly felt that shift.

In unstable moments, consistency becomes leadership' s greatest asset.

Day 10 – 9th March: The First Turning Point

Ten days in, yes, ten days.

It doesn't sound like much when you say it out loud, but it feels like far more, ten days since the first disruption, ten days since the sounds that didn't belong, ten days of adjusting, observing, holding steady and today, for the first time, a different question settled in my mind:

Is this moving towards something long-term?

That thought didn't arrive with urgency; it arrived quietly, but it stayed and what began as a disruption now feels embedded, not normal, not acceptable, but familiar and that familiarity carries its own weight.

The news this morning didn't bring reassurance; if anything, it carried more substance, more intent, less speculation and more direction. The language has shifted, and with it, the sense that this is not resolving as quickly as many had hoped. You could feel that in conversations today, the first day back at work from the weekend.

"This will pass soon "became diluted and more of "we need to prepare."

At home, I noticed it more than anywhere else: conversations with family have changed; questions that didn't exist a week ago are now being asked more openly, not out of fear, but out of awareness.

"Is everything okay?"
"Is this going to continue?"
"What do we need to do if it gets worse?"

You find yourself answering carefully, not to avoid the truth but to protect the space around them, to keep a sense of normality where you can, even when you know things are shifting.

There's a responsibility in that, not just to lead at work, but to lead at home, and sometimes, that's the harder place to stay steady.

I've changed too, I can feel it, outwardly I don't want to admit to it, but subconsciously I became less reactive, more measured, more aware of what matters and what doesn't.

The unnecessary noise falls away quickly in moments like this, and what remains is clarity.

There's also a quiet acceptance forming, not resignation but recognition that this isn't passing quickly and once that becomes clear, something shifts in how you lead.

This is no longer about reacting to a crisis; this is about enduring through it, and endurance requires something deeper, not energy that fades, not urgency that burns out, but something more sustainable. It's about clarity so people know where they stand, consistency, so nothing feels unstable unnecessarily, care so people know they are not carrying this alone and above all, presence, a steady presence even when the ground feels anything but steady, because by Day 10, people are no longer just looking for reassurance, they are looking for signals of what comes next, and whether we realize it or not they are watching how we carry ourselves to find it.

What today taught me:

There comes a point when uncertainty stops feeling temporary and, in that moment, leadership must shift from reaction to endurance, the moment you realise this will last is the moment leadership must change.

The First Shift

What the First Ten Days Revealed

Ten days.

On paper, it doesn't seem significant, a short period, a brief disruption, but lived in real time, it becomes something else entirely.

The first ten days are not defined by events alone; they are defined by how those events are felt, what begins as curiosity quietly becomes awareness, and what feels temporary begins to settle into something more permanent. What is distant gradually becomes personal, and somewhere in between, people begin to change.

In those first moments, it is the unfamiliar that unsettles, a sound that doesn't belong, a silence where there should be noise, a headline that interrupts routine.

At first, the mind searches for logic, common sense, that this will pass, this won't last.

But as the days unfold, that certainty begins to weaken, and questions replace assumptions.

"How long will this go on?"

"What if it escalates?"

"What does this mean for us?"

And when those questions arrive, they don't just sit in the mind, they enter the home, because uncertainty is not experienced in isolation, it follows you through the front door, it sits in conversations with family, the pauses between words and in the questions asked more carefully than before.

"Is everything okay?"

"What do we need to do?"

And in those moments, leadership takes on a different meaning, not the leadership of strategy or decision-making, but the leadership of presence, of holding a tone, of protecting a sense of normality, of carrying concern without passing it on.

At work, leadership is visible; at home, it is felt, and often, it is harder.

Across these ten days, something else becomes clear. People do not respond to uncertainty in the same way; some seek information, some withdraw, some speak more, some say very little at all. But beneath those differences, there is a shared need, not for perfect answers, but for steadiness. The instinct in leadership is often to act, to provide clarity, to give direction, to resolve uncertainty.
But more noticeable, the first ten days teach a different lesson, not all uncertainty can be resolved, some of it must simply be held, and in those moments, leadership is not about control, it is about consistency, same tone, same presence, no unnecessary change. Because when everything else feels unstable, people look for what remains steady, and over time, that steadiness becomes something more powerful than certainty; it becomes trust.

There is also a quieter lesson, one that reveals itself slowly. Resilience does not arrive dramatically; it builds in repetition in people continuing to show up, continuing to work, continuing to care for one another, not because things are easy but because stopping is not an option.

By **Day 10**, something shifts towards, *"How do we continue if it doesn't get resolved?"*
This is the first shift, the first real turning point, because that question changes everything.
It moves leadership from reaction to endurance, from short-term response to long-term responsibility.

What these first ten days reveal is simple, but not easy: when certainty disappears, people look for:

Clarity, to understand where they stand.
Consistency, to feel stability.
Care, to know they are not alone.

And above all:

Presence.
A steady presence.
Not loud.
Not dramatic.
But constant.

Because in uncertain times, it is not always answers that sustain people, it is how others show up around them, it defined the foundation, revealed the character, tests composure and exposes what truly matters. Once this turning point is passed, you will not return unchanged; you will move forward differently, more aware, more measured and more intentional. The harsh reality is that you no longer look for a resolution; you just wait for what comes next.
These first ten days were not the end of uncertainty; it was the moment we understood it had only just begun.

Day 11 – 10th March: When positions begin to form

By now, the language had changed, not in a way that demanded attention; it wasn't a dramatic shift, nor was it enough to stop you in your tracks, but just enough to notice. It was, in my view, only the kind of shift that reveals itself slowly, in repeated phrases, in the tone behind the words, in what is said, and what is no longer being said.

Official statements felt firmer, less cautious, where the early uncertainty, where every word seemed carefully balanced, had begun to give way to something more deliberate. There was structure to news, to conversations, and now there was a definitive intent, a sense that positions were no longer being formed, but were already forming.

I wouldn't call this escalation, but more directional, and that distinction mattered in terms of engaging with people, unifying, projecting resilience as to who we are and what we stand for in the UAE.
At ground level, you could feel it too, not through announcements or headlines but through people, conversations had changed, they were no longer just reactive, no longer centered around what is happening, as if the answer might still be simple and contained, instead, they had started to stretch, people were making their own interpretations, joining the dots, filling in gaps where information didn't yet exist. Trying to make sense of something that no longer felt distant enough to be observed passively.

With that came something else, assumptions, not intentional, not careless, but human, where emotions started to sit alongside information, yes, it was their own personal perspective blending with partial understanding, some of which were totally off the radar, the mind, naturally, trying to create certainty or uncertainty, where none had been fully given.

You could hear it in the way people spoke, there was more conviction, less hesitation, but not necessarily with more clarity, and still, on the surface, there was calm.

Work continued, routines held, the city moved in the way it always had but it wasn't the same calm, it didn't settle you in the same way because underneath it, something had shifted, the calm no longer came from confidence, it came from control, a controlled tone, a controlled environment, a controlled attempt to hold steady what was quietly beginning to move.

And that's when you realize, calm can exist, even when certainty does not, clarity does not always comfort, sometimes it simply carries weight.

Day 12 – 11th March: *When clarity carried weight*

Clarity began to surface, not all at once, not in a way that answered everything, but enough to shift the ground beneath us, and with it came something unexpected, not reassurance, if anything, the opposite, because the more information that emerged, the harder it became to hold onto the idea that this was temporary.

What once felt like a disruption now revealed itself as something more layered, more deliberate. Movements were unfolding beyond what we could see, beyond what was being openly shared, but enough signals, enough consistency, to understand this was not incidental.

This whole situation had shape, it had what seemed to be a predetermined structure, and that realization carried weight. On the surface, the day passed without incident, no defining moment, no escalation or even dare I say, de-escalation that demanded attention. But internally, it didn't feel quiet because silence, by now, no longer meant calm, something had shifted, assumption had been replaced, and, in its place, stood understanding, not complete, not comfortable, but enough to change how you carried the day because once you begin to understand even partially, you can no longer retreat into uncertainty.

This new mindset, way of thinking, helped to see patterns, you actually start to begin to anticipate, you begin to feel the edges of what might come next, and that's when it settles in.

This isn't just happening around us; it is unfolding with intent, and understanding that is far heavier than not knowing at all.

Day 13 – 12th March: When the outside world steps in

Something shifted today, not in what we could immediately see, but in how it was being carried beyond us. Until now, it had felt contained, not controlled, but held within a space we could still define. The conversations, the reactions, the focus, they all lived close to home, even when the reality suggested otherwise, there was still a sense that this was something happening to us, within a boundary we could recognize.

Unfortunately, that boundary began to dissolve, the tone widened, not abruptly but steadily. International voices, once occasional, became consistent; statements no longer felt like observations from a distance, they started to carry position, alignment and interpretation. The language stretched beyond immediate events into something broader.

This wasn't just a war of words, we all felt it, it was now loaded with economic implications, regional stability, longer-term consequences words that don't belong to moments, words that belong to timelines, and for many us, that's when it started to feel different because when something is discussed in terms of impact, not just an event or historical timeline, it signals something deeper, something that isn't passing through, something that is beginning to take shape beyond its origin.

You could feel it in how people spoke, there was a shift in posture, not physical, but mental, less focus on the immediate, more awareness of the wider picture.
People weren't just reacting to what was happening anymore they were trying to understand where it sat in something larger, and with that came a subtle unease, because this was no longer just ours, the crisis was being watched, interpreted, positioned, responded to from places we couldn't see, by people we wouldn't hear directly, but whose influence was already shaping the direction of what came next.

That's the turning point, and that changes how something and someone feels because when the outside world steps in, the stakes change, the narrative expands, the outcome becomes less about a single place, a single moment, and more about how it connects, how it spreads, how it settles across borders.

So today felt bigger, heavier. less contained, and that's the moment you realize this is no longer just something happening within reach, it is something unfolding beyond it, and once it reaches that point, it doesn't return to where it started. Was this the starting point for how the world may change, how people's perception of safety may change?

As I theme leadership throught these pages, I start to see that he longer uncertainty stays, the more discipline leadership requires. This is no longer a test of the most successful leaders, it's a test of steadfastness, and the ability to keep developing the 'A' class players you have in your team, theres no time to have 'B or C' class players in moments like this.

Day 14 – 13th March: The silence between the warnings

By day fourteen, it wasn't the noise that unsettled you anymore; it was the silence that followed it, not calm, not peace, but a silence that asked questions you couldn't answer, the kind that makes you listen harder, the kind that makes you hold your breath without realizing it.

In the early days, everything felt sudden, almost chaotic, bursts of sound, flashes of updates, a rush of uncertainty that came and went in waves, but now this felt different, like really different, it felt more measured, more intentional, as if what was unfolding had found its rhythm, and that rhythm, which no one embraced, was relentless.

Unfamiliar noises still marked the sky, alerts still broke through the day without warning, but what settled in today wasn't fear in its loudest form, it was the waiting, waiting between alerts, waiting for the next vibration of your phone, waiting for clarity that never quite arrived, only fragments, interpretations, half-truths stitched together into something that still didn't feel whole.

We all know that the human mind doesn't like gaps, and because of this, it fills them with assumptions, with imagined scenarios, with quiet fears that grow louder in the absence of certainty.

At home, this waiting had a presence of its own.

You could feel it in the way conversations paused mid-sentence, in the way the television stayed on longer than usual, not for entertainment, but for reassurance, in the way children looked up, not always asking questions, but searching faces for answers, and that's where it hits you most, because in that moment, you are not just experiencing this as an individual, you are carrying it for others, as a parent, as a partner, as the one who is expected to translate uncertainty into calm.

You even find yourself softening your tone, choosing language carefully, balancing truth with protection.

"Everything is okay, we are in a safe place", words that leave your mouth before your mind fully agrees, because leadership at home is not about having the answers, it's about holding the space when there are none, and that takes something deeper than confidence, it takes restraint, it takes emotional discipline, it takes absorbing your own uncertainty so it doesn't spill into those who look to you for steadiness.

Then you step into work and realize the same dynamic exists, just dressed differently, meetings resumed, calendars filled again, decisions still need to be made.

On the surface, structure had returned, but underneath there was a quiet recalibration happening in every room, conversations became more intentional, less speculation, more precision, people spoke when they had something meaningful to say, not just to fill space.

Leaders, especially, carried a different weight today; you could see it in their posture, hear it in their tone, the careful framing of every message, because this wasn't just about performance anymore, this was about presence, being strong without pretending everything was under control, and perhaps that was the hardest balance of all.

It felt that somewhere between home and work, between family and leadership, a truth became impossible to ignore, the mindset moved from when will this end, to how do we sustain ourselves through this, how do we create stability when everything feels fluid.

Day 15 – 14th March: The Karma of Endurance

There's a moment in any crisis when resilience stops being something you reach for and becomes something you live, day fifteen felt like that moment, the notifications still came, the distant sounds still echoed across the sky, and yes, in reality nothing had really changed externally, but people had, movements were calmer now, more deliberate, almost as if life had found a rhythm within the disruption, and that, in itself, is a confronting realization.

It wasn't that fear had disappeared; trust me, it hadn't, it had simply taken a quieter seat within us, less visible, still deep within our subconscious, but still present. At home, the shift was subtle but undeniable. Children asked fewer questions, not because they understood more, but because they were learning what normal now looked like, and as adults, we spoke less in reassurances. It was like an unspoken understanding that constant reassurance no longer settled the moment.

Instead, we offered presence, consistency, a steady tone in an unsteady time, because leadership at home had evolved; it was no longer about protecting people from reality, it was about helping them stand within it.

At work, the same pattern unfolded: fewer reactive conversations, more grounded decisions, less noise, more intent. People were no longer asking, "What's happening?" They were asking, "What do we do next?"

In that shift alone, something deeper revealed itself, karma, not in the mystical sense, but in the very real, human way. What we gave our attention to began to shape our experience. If we fed fear, it grew; if we fed stability, it anchored us. The energy we brought into rooms, into homes, into conversations didn't disappear; it circulated, it multiplied, it returned, and so, almost instinctively, people began choosing differently. They began to choose calm over panic, structure over chaos, showing up, even when it felt heavy, even humor started to emerge, not careless, not dismissive, but necessary, described as a quiet rebellion against the weight of it all, a reminder that even in uncertainty, we still had some control over how we felt, and in that, there was something powerful, recalibration, where we find balance, even when the ground beneath us isn't steady.

But Day fifteen also carried a quiet warning: what we normalize today will shape who we become tomorrow. Resilience, when left unchecked, can harden our approach. So today wasn't just about adapting, it was about stabilizing, choosing, consciously, the kind of environment we create, for our families, for our teams, for ourselves.

Because in the middle of all this, one truth became clear: we may not control what is happening around us, but we are still responsible for what we build within it. Endurance is quiet, but it is where real leadership lives.

Day 16 – 15th March: When endurance becomes the reality

By day sixteen, something settled in that no one had planned for; it wasn't fear, nor was it shock, but what it was was duration. The quiet, undeniable realization that this was not passing through us, we were now living within it.

The early questions had disappeared: how long will this last, and when will it stop?

These no longer held the same urgency, because somewhere along the way, the answer had already begun to form that this isn't short-term, and that understanding was packaged alongside something heavier than uncertainty and that was fatigue, not the kind sleep fixes, not the kind you shake off with a good night's rest, but emotional fatigue, the kind that sits behind your eyes, the kind that slows your reactions, softens your sharpness, stretches your patience.

Fatigue started to show itself in the smallest ways, delayed responses in conversations, sometimes a moment longer to process something simple, and pauses lingered just a second or more to process. You could look into people's eyes, they may have looked present, but they carried something deeper.

At home, it was quieter, not because things were calm, but because the energy and life dynamics had changed; there was less questioning and less explaining. Families sitting together, not always speaking, but sharing the same space and the same weight, and this is where you started to notice how people were conserving themselves, for the long haul, because somewhere inside, everyone was managing their own reserve.

At work, the same pattern unfolded, performance hadn't dropped, if anything, people were still delivering, leaders were carrying a different kind of strain, not visible like breakdowns, but you could see this became a constant balancing act, leaders were offering direction, even when clarity was incomplete, holding strength, while allowing just enough honesty to remain human, because people weren't just looking for answers anymore, they were looking for stability, and stability, in moments like this, doesn't come from certainty, it comes from consistency, from how you show up, from the tone you set, from the energy you bring into every room, every conversation, every home.

There was now a feeling about how to sustain people through something ongoing, through something that doesn't yet have a clear edge and that shift where it doesn't announce itself loudly, it doesn't come with a defining moment, it settles in quietly, but once you feel it, which we all were, you can't unsee it. Because from this point forward, it's no longer about reacting well, it's about enduring well, and the difference between the two, is where real leadership begins to show

Day 17 – 16th March: When perspective finds you again

Something shifted today, not in the skies, not in the headlines, but within people.

It wasn't optimism, it wasn't relief, it was perspective, the kind that doesn't arrive loudly but settles quietly, after enough has been seen, felt, and carried.

By day seventeen, the question had changed again: "What will this leave behind?" was becoming an echo across numerous discussions.

At work, you could feel it in conversations, not in formal meetings, but in the spaces between them. A senior leader, usually focused on numbers and delivery, paused mid-discussion and said, "We've spent years building plans for growth and profit, but how do we build people who can carry this", it wasn't a strategy question, it was a human one and for the first time in days, that question wasn't brushed aside, it was answered with the utmost honesty, because something had softened, not weakness but awareness.

At home, the shift was even more visible; families were no longer just gathering out of necessity, they were choosing to stay close, conversations stretched longer, and phones were put down more often, not out of discipline, but because presence had become more valuable than distraction.

I watched children today, not playing out of escape, but out of instinct, adapting games around what was happening, turning uncertainty into imagination, and adults began to sit differently, less restless, more grounded because something inside had adjusted.

There was a quiet acceptance forming.

Not of the situation itself, but of the fact that this moment was shaping us, whether we resisted it or not.

Even small acts carried more meaning, was this because of acceptance because even at this point, the crisis hadn't disappeared, but its grip had changed, it was no longer just something happening to us, it was beginning to work through us, shaping how we think, how we connect, how we lead, and perhaps most importantly how we choose to show up for one another.

Of course, there was still uncertainty, still disruption, still no clear end, but alongside it, something else had emerged, clarity of a different kind, an understanding that when this eventually passes, and it will, we won't return as we were, because moments like this don't just test people, they redefine them, reshape their thinking and perspective, and that shift, quiet, almost invisible in real time may one day be the part we look back on where such a crisis like this, just reshapes everything.

Day 18 – 17th March: *Living within It*

I woke early today to the distant sound of those now familier noise. Familiar has now become part of the early morning rhythm. But today felt different. Noticeably quieter in one way I didn't hear any flighst today

A quick glance at the news confirmed it!

"The airspace is closed due to emergency safety measures."

That was the moment it shifted. Not just the noise, but something internal. For the first time since February 28th, I felt a sense of uncertainty about the days and weeks ahead.

The drive to work was as it has been lately, light traffic, quiet streets, almost deceptively, yet beneath it all, a tension sat quietly, refusing to leave.
Inside the office, it was clear no one had slept through it untouched. Conversations carried fragments of the morning, shaking windows, the smell of smoke through AC vents, the thunderous sounds closer than comfort allows. Real experiences, spoken calmly, but heavy with meaning, and still, we showed up.

We stood firm, we worked as normal. By now, the question had changed; it was no longer if this would continue, but how long and in what way.
Planning reflected conversations that stretched further ahead, and there was less focus on immediate disruption and more on sustained adjustment. You realized that what once felt temporary was becoming part of the landscape. The closer uncertainty feels, the more intentional leadership must become.

Day 19 – 18th March: The Weight of Continuation

Last night was different, not in the way the previous nights had been distant sounds, faint disruptions, moments that could still be rationalized or pushed to the edges of thought.

This was something else; the sky lit up, for the first time since this began, it wasn't just sound or speculation. It was visible, immediate, impossible to ignore.

Light cut across the darkness in sharp, sudden bursts, the kind that makes you stop mid-thought, mid-movement, and for a moment, the night didn't feel like night anymore; it felt exposed. There was no confusion about what was happening, no need to check the news or wait for confirmation; you could see it, you could feel it, and for the first time, it felt close.

The sounds followed louder, heavier, more frequent, not the distant echoes we had grown used to, but something more defined, more deliberate.

There was a moment, brief but real, where time seemed to pause. People stepped outside, looking upward, not out of curiosity, but out of instinct, trying to understand what they were witnessing, even if there were no words for it.

Phones lit up almost instantly. Messages. Calls. Questions without answers.

"Are you seeing this?"
"Where is it?"
"Is everyone okay?"

Inside, there was a shift I hadn't felt before, not panic, but something closer to it than we had allowed ourselves to experience in the days leading up to this. Until now, much of this had been processed at a distance, managed through routine, balanced with logic, and, in a subconscious way, contained. Last night certainly broke that distance; it brought the situation into view, and sleep, when it came, was light and interrupted. Every sound now notably carried more weight, and for now, every silence felt temporary.

This morning, the city moved again as it always does, cars on the roads, and some offices were open as working from home almost resonated with the 2020 COVID-19 times. But something had changed; you could see it in the way people spoke, slower, more deliberate, with less assumption that things would quickly return to normal. The questions were different today, trying to fathom out how far it might go.

At work, I felt the need to be more present than ever, even with work from home, not to explain because there was little to explain but to steady the room to steady the thoughts, to retrench people's emotions. It became clear in moments like this test more than systems or plans, they test composure, the ability to carry composure without passing it on.

I realized those who looked at me for support required focus on what we could control, clarity where possible, calm where needed and space for people to process what they had experienced, because last night wasn't just an event, it was a marker, a stick in the sand, line between what this had been… and what it might become, and once that line is crossed, you don't go back to viewing things the same way again.

What today taught me:
There are moments when uncertainty becomes visible, and in those moments, leadership is measured not by what you say, but by how you carry yourself.

Day 20 – 19th March: The Quiet before what should have been joy

Today carried a weight that felt different, not louder, not more violent, but heavier in a way that settled deep rather than shook the surface.

It was the final day of Ramadan; under any other circumstances, this day would hum with anticipation. Messages would already be flying back and forth, invitations being made, plans forming. There would be a shared sense of gratitude, of completion, of something earned through patience and reflection, the kind of energy that gently builds toward Eid.

But today, that energy never came; instead, there was a stillness, not peace but restraint.
Twenty days into this conflict, and for the first time, it felt like the absence of normality was louder than the disruption itself. The early morning had already reminded us of those interceptions overhead, distant noises that have now become part of the rhythm we never asked for.
Conversations today weren't about plans or gatherings; they were quieter, more measured, people spoke, but with less certainty, less assumption about tomorrow. It struck me how quickly a society can adapt on the surface, while internally still searching for something solid to hold onto.

Eid is around the corner, but it doesn't feel close; there's no clear "light at the end", just a continuation, a question mark stretching into what should have been a celebration, and yet, there is something else, too. Resilience, perhaps, but not the loud, defiant kind, a quieter form, people still showing up, still holding routines together, even when the meaning behind those routines feels altered.

Maybe that's what leadership looks like in moments like this, not certainty, not answers, but presence. The ability to stand in the unknown and still create a sense of steadiness for others, I feel that today wasn't defined by what happened, it was defined by what didn't and somehow, that made it one of the most significant days so far.

Days 1–20: *The distance that disappeared*

Nothing could have mapped out these first 20 days; it really didn't arrive with clarity.
There was no defining moment you could point to and say that's when everything changed.
Just a sound that didn't belong, distant, unfamiliar, easy at first to digest, to question, then it became harder to ignore.

In the early days, it lived on the edges, in headlines you read twice, in conversations that started, paused, then restarted again, in the quiet habit of checking your phone more often than you needed to. It was present but not yet personal, there was still space between us and it and for a while, that space gave us comfort. But space has a way of closing, not suddenly, not dramatically, just enough, each day, that you begin to notice what's missing. The familiar rhythm of flights overhead, the ease in conversations, the assumption that tomorrow would feel like yesterday and when those small things shift, you realize something larger already has.

By the second week, it had moved closer, no longer something you observed, but something you felt in the way people spoke, calm but heavier. In the stories that didn't need embellishment, windows shaking, sleep interrupted, the kind of details that sit with you longer than they should, and still, we carried on, we went to work, we held routines together, we showed up. Because in moments like this, routine becomes more than a habit; it becomes your anchor. Then the questions changed, quietly, but completely; it was no longer what was happening? It became, how long does this last?

That shift doesn't just change conversation, it changes mindset, plans stretch further than comfort allows, thoughts move ahead of the present, and somewhere within you, without fully acknowledging it, you begin to prepare for something that doesn't yet have a shape.

Then came the moment that removed all distance, not imagined, not reported or seen.
The sky no longer held it at arm's length; it brought it forward into view, into focus, into something you could no longer process from afar. Light was cutting through darkness, sound that didn't echo but arrived and, in that moment, something inside you adjusts, not panic, but close enough to recognize that things will not be processed the same way again.

After that, even the silence changes, sleep becomes lighter, stillness feels temporary, calm no longer reassures, it just waits, almost in a stealth-like manner.

By **Day 20**, it isn't the noise that defines it; it's what's missing. The final days of Ramadan should have carried warmth, anticipation, connection, a quiet build toward something shared, something certain, but instead, there was restraint, a stillness that didn't settle the mind but held it, and that absence was louder than anything that came before it.

This is what twenty days feels like, not a timeline, a transition, from watching to feeling, from feeling to understanding, from understanding to living within it, and yet, in all of this, something remains, not loud, not visible at first glance, but constant.

People still show up, still carry on, still find a way to move forward, even when forward is unclear, not through certainty but through presence, because somewhere between Day 1 and Day 20, you stop waiting for it to end, not because hope disappears, but because reality settles, and once that happens you don't return to who you were at the beginning, you move forward as someone who has seen it, felt it, and now, lives within it.

Day 21 – 20th March: Eid between two worlds

"Joy interrupted, but not broken."

Eid Mubarak echoed softly through the morning as the sun began to rise, a familiar warmth settling over homes, streets, and hearts. There was something different in the air today, not silence, but intention. Families were waking with purpose, children already restless with excitement, messages flowing, calls being made, doors opening.

For a moment, it felt whole again, homes filled quickly, laughter returned in fragments at first, then fully, as if it had been waiting just beneath the surface all along. Tables prepared, hands shaken, embraces held just a second longer than usual. You could feel it; this wasn't just a celebration, it was reassurance, a quiet, collective agreement to show up for one another, being together as one.

Then, as it has become all too familiar, the sky reminded us of a distant sound, not loud enough to cause panic, but not soft enough to ignore. Conversations paused mid-sentence, eyes lifted, instinctively, and that brief moment where everyone silently asks the same question, was that what I think it was?

It didn't take long for reality to settle back in. There was something particularly difficult about it today. Not fear, but confusion, why today, why now, on a morning meant for peace, reflection, and unity, where the thought passed through many minds, unspoken but shared.

I've tried to keep politics out of these pages, to stay grounded in what is felt rather than what is argued, but today tested that boundary, not in anger, but in a deeper questioning of purpose, of timing, of impact, and when moments like this are disrupted, it's not strategy you feel, it's intrusion into something human.

Yet, despite it, something else stood stronger; families stayed, and conversations resumed. Children continued to play, plates were passed, laughter, though briefly shaken, returned, not forced, but chosen; there was resilience in that choice. Solidarity wasn't a concept today, it was visible in the way people remained present, in the way they refused to let a moment be taken from them entirely.

For a few hours, there was something close to normal again, not the absence of conflict, but the presence of unity, and perhaps that's what stayed with me most.

Not the interruption, but the response to it.

I learned each day, that leadership is not about removing uncertainty, it' s about carrying others through it, anchoring positive thoughts, demonstrating resilience throughout no matter how hard it seemed at the time, this needed to be displayed.

Day 22 – 21st March: The storm between two realities

Eid still lingers and yet you can feel it in the quieter moments, the softened pace, the faint echoes of celebration that haven't fully left us. There's still something gentle in the air, something that tries to remind us of normality, even if only briefly. But today began differently, the sky didn't behave as it had in recent weeks, there were no familiar interceptions carving through the morning, no distant rhythm we had reluctantly learned to live with. Instead, there was a stillness and then a darkness.

At first, it felt almost out of place, rain, this late in the season? A strange thought to hold onto, given everything else, and then it came, thunder, sudden and unapologetic, lightning stretching across the sky, splitting it open and within moments, the heavens followed.
Rain fell with intent, sideways, driven by winds that didn't ease but pushed harder, roads disappeared beneath water, pavements blurred into reflections. The city, so used to control and structure, gave way in minutes to something raw and uncontained, and yet, it was beautiful.

For a brief moment, the air felt different, clean, perhaps a reset of the weight we've been carrying, if only for minutes; it lifted, it was surreal, not because of the storm itself, but because of what it interrupted. The familiar tension, the quiet readiness, the background noise of a crisis we have slowly adapted to, all paused. But only briefly, because beneath that moment of calm, something else has been building. The intensity of the crisis feels lower on the surface now, less immediate, less sharp, and yet, the conversations tell a different story.

People aren't just watching anymore, they're preparing, not loudly, not dramatically, but deliberately. Questions are being asked that didn't exist even a few days ago:

Have you packed an emergency bag?
Do you have money set aside, just in case?
Where are your passports? Can you reach them instantly?

These aren't questions of panic; they are questions of acceptance, an understanding, perhaps unspoken, that this may not pass quickly, that what we are living through could stretch across time, across borders, across lives far beyond our own immediate view, and that's when it shifts from something we are experiencing to something we are beginning to live within.

You start to see it in people, some carry worry more visibly now, their thoughts racing ahead of the present, others stand with a quiet strength, more composed than before as if something within them has settled into place, and then there are those moments, in between conversations, where the questions linger just a little too long, not fear, but awareness.

What I see and feel now is a definitive recognition that the human landscape is changing, not overnight, not dramatically but steadily, with each passing day, and still, Eid lingers, a reminder of togetherness, of faith, of hope, so we hold tight onto that, we look, we wait, we hope, and perhaps more than anything, we pray that this does not become the rhythm we carry forward.

But, and I say this out loud, no matter what happens, I felt I was surrounded with safety, reassurance, resilience, a feeling that no other place could offer such safety. Stand your ground, be loyal, be proud of where you are and what you are surrounded by echoed through my mind.

Day 23 – 22nd March: The calm that questions itself

Eid has now passed, and the softness it brought, even in the middle of everything, has begun to fade. What remains is a slow return to routine, people preparing to go back to work, conversations shifting back to schedules, priorities and deliverables, as if structure might help restore a sense of control.

But it's not the same return, children are now being schooled from home, not out of disruption, but precaution, a decision that speaks quietly, but clearly, one that doesn't need explanation, because everyone understands what sits behind it.

Yes, we are adjusting again, today, on the surface, felt almost normal, the skies were quieter than we've grown used to, fewer interruptions, less intensity, synchronizing into the kind of day that, not long ago, would have passed without a second thought, and yet, that's what made it feel different because normal no longer settles the mind the way it used to, it actually questions it.

There's a tension in quieter days now, not relief, but suspicion; some would describe it as the lull before the storm. A sense that the absence of activity doesn't necessarily mean safety, but pause, it is a moment between movements. The news didn't help settle anything. The language has shifted again, stronger now, less measured, with words that carry further, that hint at wider implications, broader reach, consequences that extend beyond what we've already seen, not immediate, not defined, but enough to stretch the imagination beyond comfort.

I question whether this is where true anxiety lives, what I ask, not in what is happening, but rather, what might. You actually begin to feel it in people, a return to work, but with a different energy, focus is there but thinner, more fragile, conversations are shorter, but heavier, people are present but part of them is elsewhere, quietly scanning, quietly processing, and what's most unsettling is not the intensity of the day, it's the contrast, because I now feel that after everything we've experienced, a quieter day should bring relief, but it doesn't fully, it leaves space, a void, and in that space, the mind fills in what it doesn't know, which is back to where I started, this is anxiety.

Yet, we continue, we adapt, we move forward in the way people always do.

But beneath that movement, there is a growing awareness, subtle, but steady, that this is no longer something that simply happens around us, it is shaping how we think, how we plan, how we prepare and perhaps that's the quiet truth of today, life will never be the same and life will now take theses scars and bruises where not every shift comes with noise, some will now come in the silence.

Day 24 – 23rd March: *When the sky changed the story*

Today was different, not because of the war, but because something far more immediate, far more human, took hold of us all, and that was the sky itself.

The warnings had come early, forecasts spoke with an unusual certainty, a quiet authority that something significant was coming, heavy rain, they said, perhaps even record-breaking, the kind of rain the UAE does not forget, and for once, they were right.

By 11:00 am, the sky opened without hesitation, not a gentle fall, not a passing shower, but a relentless, unapologetic downpour, the kind that drowns out thought, the kind that forces you to stop, to look, to reassess and take immediate action. By 1:00 pm, the roads had begun to surrender, water pooled, became lakes in the roads and then, without stopping, it surged into an unstoppable force. Familiar routes became uncertain paths, movement slowed, then stalled, and in that moment, something shifted across the country. For the first time in weeks, the war stepped back, not because it ended but because something closer demanded our attention.

Business continuity plans were activated almost instinctively, organizations moving with precision, not out of fear of conflict, but out of responsibility for people. Safety became immediate, tangible, visible; leaders didn't need to remind anyone what mattered. Everyone already knew, and believe me, there was something quietly powerful in that, which I best describe as an unifying force, not driven by headlines or geopolitics, but by shared humanity and humility. Everyone was checking on colleagues, calling family, helping strangers navigate flooded roads. The crisis had changed shape, and so had we.

Even the sounds above us blurred into something else; what once triggered tension, those distant echoes in the sky became uncertain. Was it thunder? Was it something more? And for the first time, we hesitated not out of fear, but out of ambiguity, and strangely, that ambiguity felt softer.

As the day stretched on, another whisper began to circulate, ceasefire, a word we had almost forgotten how to receive. Cautiously, it moved through conversations with quizzical questions such as, was it real, was it temporary, maybe a pause, or a strategy? No one truly knew, and yet, something undeniable began to happen; the emotional weight shifted, not dramatically, not all at once, but enough to create a light, a glimmer of hope.

Anxiety loosened its grip, conversations softened, the constant edge that had defined our days dulled, even if only slightly. Hope, fragile and unfamiliar, began to find its way back in, and perhaps that was the most powerful moment of all, not the rain, not the disruption, not even the rumors of peace, but the reminder that even in the most uncertain of times, something can change suddenly, unexpectedly and with it, the way we feel, the way we think, the way we carry ourselves forward.

Tonight, we didn't celebrate certainty; we sat with possibility, and for now, that was enough, where the sky had, without doubt, changed the story, and when everything else shifts, routine becomes stability

Day 25 – 24th March: When strength reveals the cracks

The rain had finally stepped back after Monday's relentless downpour, the kind that blurred roads and tested patience; the city felt almost paused, quieter, lighter, as if catching its breath. The roads were clearer now, less resistance, less chaos; it should have felt like relief, but something had shifted.

It was still officially a work-from-home day, yet I couldn't stay still, there was an usual get up and go urge I have, almost instinctive, to return to the office, to sit at my desk, to move, to act, to hold on to routine as if it were a form of control in a world that had slowly become unpredictable.

So, I went in, the journey felt different, calmer on the outside, but internally, something had hardened. The news played in the background, as it had every day, but now it was no longer shocking; it had become a daily ritual, listening, absorbing, filtering, because not everything was the truth anymore. The lines between fact, assumption, and noise had blurred so much that you had no choice but to become your own gatekeeper. International voices grew louder, opinions multiplied, and somewhere in between it all, clarity became something you had to fight for, and that in itself was exhausting.

At work, there was a moment I've come to value more than most: time with senior leaders. It's where reality tends to surface, not in presentations or structured updates, but in tone, in pauses, in the things left unsaid, but today felt different; the conversations carried weight, not panic, not overt fear, but something subtler, something more telling.
Concern had crept in, the kind that speaks not just about today, but about what lies ahead, economic uncertainty, longer-term implications, the quiet acknowledgement that this may not pass as quickly as we once hoped, and for the first time, I saw it clearly.

Even the strongest voices had moments of hesitation; that's when you realize leadership is not about having all the answers, it's about holding the line when others begin to question it. It's about stepping forward, not because you are unaffected, but because others need you to be steady, and when leaders begin to carry visible weight, that is the moment you pick up the baton, you focus, you simplify, you act within your control, you become the calm others are searching for. Because the truth we often overlook is this, the higher you rise, the quieter it becomes; there are fewer places to offload, fewer people to turn to without consequence and in that silence, even the strongest leaders feel the strain; they are not immune, they are human, and perhaps that was the most powerful lesson of today.

Strength is not the absence of pressure; it is the ability to carry it, even when it begins to show. This isn't just about leadership in business; it's about life because the same signals exist everywhere, in our homes, in our children, in our parents, in our friends. The strongest among them will rarely say when they are struggling, you have to see it, feel it, notice the subtle shifts and when you do, you respond with patience, with presence, with empathy.

Day 25 reminded me of something simple, yet easy to forget: no one is unbreakable and sometimes, the greatest strength we can offer is not solutions, but understanding.

Day 26 – 25th March: *Hope tested; humanity unshaken*

The evening before had whispered something we had all been craving resolution.
A fragile suggestion that perhaps this would slow, perhaps this would ease, but by now, we had learned hope could no longer be taken at face value.

Every headline, every alert, every "breaking update" came with an unspoken condition: believe it carefully. From this, conversations shifted today, not louder, but heavier. Questions surrounded discussions: if talks are happening, why are we still hearing the unfamilier sounds!
If there is dialogue, why is there still destruction, and the question that lingered in every corridor, every home, every quiet pause, why us, why the UAE, a nation built on patience, on peace, on measured and visionary leadership?

No one had an answer, and perhaps that was the hardest part because as humans, we are wired for meaning; we fill gaps with stories, we connect dots that don't always belong together, just to feel some sense of control, but today, even that felt insufficient.

You could see it in leaders, not in what they said but in what they carried, the slight hesitation, the prolonged silence before responding, the weight behind their eyes. These are individuals who are built to deliver certainty, to stand as anchors, yet today, even they are being tested.
What you start to see is that beyond the walls of our immediate lives, the world seemed to echo the same instability, markets fluctuating without rhythm, oil climbing to levels that felt surreal, real estate losing its footing, airlines operating at half their capacity, skies quieter, but for all the wrong reasons.

Thirty days ago, this was nothing more than a distant ripple, a tension observed, not felt, like two fighters circling, posturing, expected, yet contained, and no one anticipated the punch would land like this.
Then, as if the day needed another layer, the skies opened again, not gently, not symbolically, but with force. Rain fell like it had something to prove, roads transformed into moving waters, cars stranded, abandoned mid-journey, signs torn from their foundations, trees broken, uprooted, it was almost like nature was mirroring the disruption we were already living. Yet, in the middle of it all, there was something quietly powerful, children playing in flooded streets as if they were beaches, laughing,

adapting, turning chaos into something almost joyful. Some were hesitant, unsure; this was new, unfamiliar, but still, they stepped into it.

As I wrote on day 25, I felt that perhaps this is what stood out most today: it wasn't the sounds from the sky, not the markets, not even the storm, but people, determined, resilient, holding onto normality, even when normal no longer made sense.

Just as the day seemed to reach its limit, another alert, another warning, a sharp reminder that even amidst floods and fatigue, the underlying tension had not left us, so what more can be said, perhaps there's nothing new, only this, that even when hope is tested, it does not disappear, it shifts, it quietens, but it stays, and tonight, like every night before, we hold onto the simplest of beliefs:

'That tomorrow must be better.'

Day 26 – 25th March

How the silence felt different from normal

The skies weren't just louder, they were filled with a display of strength, I would say more deliberate, with an intent that cuts through the sky.

Normally, aircraft overhead blends into the background with a steady rhythm you almost stop hearing as it's normal hearing them take off and land. But this was different, these weren't passing through, they were responding, they were protecting society with purpose.

What struck me more was the silence around us; there were limited commercial flights, no layered noise, just gaps and those gaps carried weight, a weight of anxiety or even surprise. For all of us, it wasn't quiet in a peaceful was it was quiet in a way that made you listen harder, where our reactions were loaded with fear, whilst wondering where the next blast would be. Would it be us, would it be close enough to scramble for protection, is all we started to think.

So, when we saw the news on the phone

I didn't panic, but others did. I paused, where others assumed the worse.

I remember the time when looking at announcements, you tended to read them twice or three times, not because I didn't understand them, but because I did. I knew deep inside that this was the moment it became real, no more speculation, no more loaded assumptions, just a confirmation of reality surrounding us all.

This became a quiet shift internally, knowing this isn't a one-off, this has structure, validation and the worst.

When driving, the roads were calm, maybe too calm.

Traffic was lighter than usual, but not in a way that felt convenient, more in a way that felt cautious. People were moving, but without urgency, almost as if everyone was present physically, but mentally somewhere else; this you could read on everyone's face and body language.

Even the environment felt different, same buildings, same routes, but for sure, the energy had changed, the flow was really different.

Arriving at work, there was no loud reaction and at work, there was a different kind of presence. People were there, but you could sense something sitting beneath the surface. Some tried to hide behind their emotions, some tried to fathom things out or read between the lines.

One thing was for sure: no one overreacted, but no one dismissed it or ignored it either.

Conversations started differently; there was less small talk.

You could tell people had experienced something, each in their own unique way, some spoke about the sounds, ohers about what they had seen or felt, windows shaking, unusual smells, disrupted sleep with noises or alert alarms and yes, for the first time, I noticed something shift, people weren't just reacting to news, they were reacting to experience, often with stories of old, anecdotes past and present.

My winning card was that I didn't allow myself to go to extremes. I didn't want to go into depths that I couldn't influence; likewise, I didn't ignore it either. There was a balance I found myself holding, acknowledging the seriousness, while staying composed, whilst listening to questions like,
How long will this last? What does this mean for work, for family, for stability? Even with these questions, I kept bringing myself back to the present. I had to control what's in front of me and stay steady, balanced and worry-free

This wasn't about suppressing emotion; it was about managing it. Letting others around feel safe, or at least know there were safe hands around them

As a leader, this is where it became clear, people looked to me differently; it was emotional content they required, not answers, but signals, how I spoke, how I carried myself, what you chose to focus on, this was. As a leader, I was very conscious of in terms of being calm but needed to be visible and present.

Clarity had to be consistent, no matter where there were uncertainties. Because in environments like this, leadership is less about direction and more about presence.

When I reflect I can say that each day wasn't the sounds reappearing, it was the shift, the realization that something had changed, even if we couldn't fully define it yet, and as days passed without escalation, it didn't feel like a normal day had been completed, it felt like the start of something and that sat with me each and every day.

My view to write this was simple, and believe me, it wasn't planned, but I felt the need to capture it before it became normal, if that would exist after. I could already sense how quickly people were adapting. How easily something significant could become routine if not acknowledged, so the writing became a way to hold onto the reality of that moment, some way to process it, to document it, not just for myself, but for what it would represent.
The beginning of something with no end in sight.

Day 27 – 26th March: When the sky lost its meaning

We all woke at the same time, not because of an alarm or notification, not because of choice, but because the night itself refused to stay quiet.

The forecasts had warned us that there would be heavy storms, record rainfall and disruption expected. We've heard that language before, we've lived through weather alerts, but nothing prepares you for when nature decides not just to arrive but to overwhelm.

The first crack of thunder didn't sound like thunder; it sounded deeper, heavier, closer to something we had come to recognize over recent weeks.

A blast echoed, then another, except this time, it rolled, stretched, echoed across the sky like it had no end. Lightning followed, not in flashes, but in sheets, lighting up the entire skyline in white, exposing everything for a split second before plunging it back into darkness. It looked like fireworks, but there was no celebration in it, just intensity, just force, and then the rain came, not the kind you watch from behind glass, the kind you hear before you see. It was relentless, dense, each drop striking with weight, building into a roar that drowned out everything else. Windows rattled, water found its way into places it had no right to be, corners of homes that had never known a leak, walls that had stood untouched for years.

It wasn't just a storm, it was pressure testing structures, testing resilience, and in the middle of it all, one question sat with every one of us:

What are we actually hearing?

Because by now, our ears had changed, over the past days, we had learned to distinguish sounds we were never meant to understand, the distant noises, the unnatural pause that follows something falling from the sky, but tonight, the storm took that clarity away.

For the first time, the sky became ambiguous, and that uncertainty was louder than any noise. Inside homes, lights flickered, phones lit up, not with alerts this time, but with messages.

"Did you hear that?"
"Was that thunder?"
"Are you okay?"

No one had answers, just shared confusion, and beneath that confusion sat something deeper, a quiet, unsettling thought. If something did happen right now, would we even know?

That's what made this night different, not the storm itself, the UAE has seen extraordinary weather before, even record-breaking rainfall in recent years, infrastructure tested, systems stretched. That part, while rare, is explainable, but layered on top of a conflict, layered on top of weeks where the sky had already become a source of tension, this was something else entirely; this was disorientation. When nature and conflict begin to sound the same, you lose more than clarity; you lose your sense of control, and emotionally, that does something to people.

Lining in a region where faith is woven into daily life, where meaning is often sought beyond the visible, it was inevitable that some would ask:

Is this a sign?

Not out of fear alone, but out of the human need to make sense of what feels beyond comprehension, and yet, as the night stretched on, something else quietly emerged, not calm, not comfort, but endurance.

We all knew that by morning, the storm would pass, the water would settle, the sky would return to its usual shade, but something had shifted because this wasn't just a night of heavy rain, it was the night the sky stopped being something we could trust to interpret, the night sound lost its certainty, the night we realized that even the familiar, can become unsettling when layered with the unknown and that realization, quiet, heavy, and deeply human stayed long after the storm had gone.

Day 28 – 27th March: When disruption becomes routine

The rain didn't just fall; it overwhelmed. Wadis that once sat quietly as part of the landscape turned into fast-moving threats, dams overflowed, roads disappeared beneath water and car parks became holding pools. Entire routes we took for granted were suddenly inaccessible, as if the city itself had paused and said, not today.

For a moment, just a moment, the crisis in the sky felt secondary, not because it had gone away, but because something more immediate had taken hold, safety, movement, survival in the most physical sense.

Businesses reacted instantly, work-from-home wasn't a precaution anymore, it was the only option, offices stood still, not by policy but by force, and with that came something deeper, a quiet disconnection, no corridor conversations, no shared glances when a distant sound made everyone pause, no collective resilience in the same room, just screens, silence, and thoughts, and in that silence, reflection grew louder.

You could feel it across conversations, calls that were no longer just about work, but about what this all means, not just here, but across the GCC. People referencing other countries, other tensions, other outcomes, the lens had widened; this was no longer local, it was regional, possibly more. Yet, despite the political statements, the press releases, the carefully constructed language used, the reality didn't shift, the unfamiliar noises didn't stop, the rhythm of disruption continued, predictable now in its unpredictability, and that's when it became clear.

This wasn't temporary behavior anymore; this was adaptation. I started noticing it in the smallest ways, conversations about holidays disappeared almost overnight, not cancelled, paused, suspended in language like,

"Let's wait until these settle."
"Maybe later in the year."
"When things go back to normal…"

But no one could define when that would be, or even what "normal" now looked like.
Schools remained closed. Distance learning extended again, another week, they said, but by now, that didn't surprise anyone. Children adapted faster than adults, screens became classrooms, homes became structured environments of learning, discipline, and quiet resilience, and we, we adjusted too.

We checked the news less emotionally, more habitually. We heard sounds in the sky and paused, but didn't panic. We carried on with meetings, decisions, responsibilities, not because things were fine, but because they had become familiar.

That's the part that stays with me the most, not the rain, not the disruption, not even the ongoing threat, but how quickly the human mind recalibrates what is acceptable, what is livable and what is normal. The question that lingered today wasn't about what was happening; it was far simpler, far heavier.

When this ends, will we even recognize normal again? My subconscious says, I doubt!

Day 29 – 28th March: *It's now real*

The sun returned today, clear. Blue, almost indifferent and beneath it, the aftermath, not the kind you associate with this part of the world, not the kind that the UAE people and visitors recognize.
Streets scattered with debris, trees and palm trees torn from roots that had held for years, bushes flattened, signage twisted, water marks still etched into walls and shop fronts. Car parks looked like abandoned scenes from somewhere else, somewhere far less predictable, far less controlled. Homeowners and shopkeepers stood outside, not in panic but in quiet repair, clearing. Lifting, resetting, there was something deeply symbolic in that, because while the storm had passed, nothing else had.

What struck me most today wasn't the damage; it was how quickly we absorbed it. Our beloved UAE, the sunshine state, with glitz, glamour and luxury, recorded rainfall levels in hours that would normally fall across months. Some areas saw over a year's worth of rain compressed into a single day. Infrastructure held in many places, flooded roads, disrupted access, businesses forced into immediate contingency, and yet within 24 hours, people were back outside, restoring what they could. That resilience, it's real, but it comes at a cost, because layered into all of this, the crisis continues, there is no pause, even as I write, today at 4 am, the windows rattled with intercepted missile blasts.

The storm didn't replace the conflict; it simply sat on top of it, and for a brief moment, the sky gave us confusion instead of clarity. Was it thunder or was it that unfamiliar sound we have gotten so use to.
Even now, that question lingers.

But the deeper shift today was not physical, it was mental, people aren't counting quiet days anymore, they're noticing patterns, frequency, timing and distance. Imagine, on February 27th, before this kicked off, I would never in my wildest dreams would have thought I would have diarorized such shocking events; they are measured occurrences.

At work, at home, in passing conversations, people are still functioning, still delivering, still showing up, but something has shifted beneath the surface. Focus requires more effort, energy is more deliberate, even optimism, feels managed, because when uncertainty stretches without a visible end, it becomes a condition, because there is no alternative.

Today didn't feel dramatic; there were no defining incidents, no sharp turns.

But it may be one of the most important days so far, because this is the day reality settled in, not loudly, not suddenly, but deeply and once it settles, everything after it is lived differently.

Day 30 – 29th March: *The 30-day line*

Thirty days, a number that sounds contained, measurable, almost manageable, but feels anything but, because in thirty days, something shifts, not just around you, but within you.

Today looked like a Sunday should, the sun rose without interruption, and the sky held its calm, uninterrupted blue. Families moved through routines that, on the surface, felt reassuringly normal: grocery runs, car washes, chores that had been postponed, then reprioritized, then quietly reabsorbed into life.

There was comfort in that rhythm, but it wasn't the same comfort as before, it was intentional, almost defiant, as if normality itself had become something we were choosing to protect, because beneath that surface, everything had changed, not dramatically, not in one defining moment, but gradually, consistently, and that is what makes it harder to confront.

Thirty days ago, this was an event; now it is an environment. The political noise continues, louder but no clearer, statements, counter-statements, posturing that feels more like performance than progress. More countries are speaking now, not always out of fear of escalation but out of fear of consequence. Because the reality is becoming harder to ignore, this is no longer just a geopolitical conflict; it is economic pressure unfolding in real time. Trade routes under scrutiny, oil price volatility beginning to ripple, airspace disruptions impacting movement, logistics and confidence, history tells us that industries don't collapse overnight; they erode, and that erosion has begun.

In conversations today, there was a noticeable shift, less focus on what is happening, more focus on what this will do.

"What happens to jobs?"
"What happens to markets?"
"What happens if this continues another month… two… three?"

No one is saying it loudly, but everyone is thinking it. Many of us have lived through disruption before, financial crises, market crashes, moments where uncertainty defined the landscape.
But this, this feels different, because it isn't sharp, it doesn't announce itself with one defining collapse, it moves slowly, quietly, almost respectfully. A slow creep into conversations, into decisions, into the way people plan or stop planning, and that is where it becomes dangerous.

Because what creeps… embeds.

At work, there is a shift from growth thinking to protection thinking. At home, it's even more visible, conversations that once looked ahead now circle around, holding steady. Children asking questions that don't have simple answers, adults answering with reassurance they are still trying to believe themselves, and then there are the questions we all ask quietly, repeatedly, almost instinctively:

Why can't this just be resolved?
Why can't people sit across a table and choose a different path?

Because what feels obvious to those living through the impact, seems distant to those shaping it and the real cost isn't just what is destroyed physically, it is what begins to form psychologically, a generation growing up hearing sounds they shouldn't recognize, understanding terms they shouldn't need to understand, normalizing a level of uncertainty that should never be normal, and yet, even with all of this, life continues.

But Day 30 draws a line, not a line of conclusion, but a line of recognition that this is not passing quickly, that this is not contained neatly, that this is shaping more than we first allowed ourselves to believe and perhaps the hardest realization of all is that we are no longer waiting for this to end, we are learning how to live while it continues.

That shift, that quiet, almost invisible acceptance, is where everything changes.

Day 31 – 30th March: Crossing the 30-day mark

We crossed the 30-day mark today, a quiet milestone but one that carried weight, and that wasn't because anything had changed, but because nothing did, because the days had continued to pass in the same suspended way, so week five has begun, and with it, a realization that is harder to ignore: there is no visible end.

Monday arrived like it always does; it was the start of a working week, routine attempting to reassert itself, trying to place familiar structure over unfamiliar circumstances, where I made my way into work, the roads still scarred from the storm, waterlogged in places, uneven, unpredictable, but passable, just enough to move forward, just enough to keep things going.

Much like everything else, inside the car, the news played on, voices, updates, statements constant, filling the space as they always do, but something had shifted, not in what was being said, but in how it was being received. There was tension now, not loud, not panicked, but present, settled beneath the surface, quiet but impossible not to notice.

At work, you could feel it before anyone spoke, in the pauses between conversations, in the way people asked questions, but didn't expect answers, because no one knew what to think anymore, not because people weren't informed but because information no longer brought clarity.

I felt this day made me realize that people have moved beyond shock, beyond reaction, into something far more difficult to manage, sustained uncertainty. I've said it before, but today it felt undeniable, the tone of language, the undercurrent of anxiety, it's changing by the hour.

One moment, there is a sense of control, then the next, quiet doubt, then a brief lift, triggered by a headline, a rumor, a possibility. Only for it to settle back into the same question:

What happens next?

People are holding onto the smallest fragments of hope now, not big declarations, not bold expectations, just fragments, a sentence, a comment, a suggestion that something might ease.

Yet the reality above us has not paused; the unfamiliar noises are still there, consistent, relentless. but now with a strange, quiet acceptance, as if repetition has made the unbearable somehow ordinary. But did something change today? They are no longer background noise, you don't just hear them, you register them, they interrupt thought, they reshape conversations, they settle into the silence between sentences, they sit in the space between words.

What we, and in particular leaders are all learning is that when uncertainty becomes constant, and disruption becomes routine, you are no longer waiting for clarity, you are learning to live without it, to move through days without expecting resolution, and that changes everything.

Reflections

A Nation That Held Its Ground

The first 30 days did not arrive with clarity. They arrived with disruption.

As I began this diary, this memoir of events, it all began with unfamiliar sounds, a sky filled with noises that no longer felt routine. The silence of commercial air traffic said more than the noise itself. It was the absence of normality that unsettled people most. In those early days, uncertainty lived in every moment, at home, on the roads, in workplaces and in schools. People searched for meaning in fragments of news, trying to understand whether this was temporary… or something far more enduring.

But what followed was not panic; it was composure, composure driven from the very core of this beautiful country – its leaders.

Across the UAE, something remarkable unfolded, not loudly, not performatively, but with quiet precision. Systems held, leadership responded, stability was not declared; it was demonstrated, pure resilience.

Workplaces remained functional, and roads, though quieter, still moved with purpose. Businesses activated continuity plans not as a reaction, but as a discipline. Even as missiles became a daily reality, no longer distant, no longer abstract, the country did not fracture under pressure; instead, it adapted, and that adaptation revealed something deeper.

Resilience within the UAE was not emotional rhetoric; it was inbred, DNA, an inherited behavior.

Families adjusted routines without losing connection. Schools shifted seamlessly into distance learning. Organisations recalibrated without losing direction. Leaders, across sectors, began to show a different kind of strength. Less visibility, more presence. Less noise, more clarity.

Because leadership, in moments like this, is not about control, it is about steadiness.

By the second and third weeks, the crisis had changed shape. It was no longer an event; it was an environment. The language people used shifted, the urgency softened into endurance. Conversations moved from "What is happening?" to "How do we sustain?"

And in that shift, something powerful emerged, "perspective".

People began to look beyond the immediate, not because the threat had disappeared, but because they had learned to live alongside it. Small moments of humanity became more visible, colleagues checked in beyond work, families gathered with intention, not obligation, and even in the middle of disruption, there was connection.

Day 24 brought storms that flooded roads and tested infrastructure, but even then, the nation responded with coordination and care. Crisis layered upon crisis did not break the system. It reinforced it.

By Day 30, the emotional weight had deepened; this was no longer about shock, it was about longevity.

The realization had settled: this would not resolve quickly, it was evident that the geopolitical noise had grown louder, economic implications were beginning to surface, leaders, for the first time, allowed concern about the future to show, not as weakness, but as awareness, and yet, even then, the UAE did not waver, because what defined these 30 days was not the conflict itself, it was the response to it.

A nation that chose steadiness over fear, a leadership approach grounded in action, not rhetoric, a society that adapted without losing its cohesion.

There was no denial of reality, but there was also no surrender to it, and that is where the true story lies, not in the number of missiles, not in the noise of the skies, but in the quiet, consistent strength shown every single day.

The UAE did not simply endure these 30 days; it absorbed them, learned from them, and continued forward, measured, composed, and united, and if the first 30 days have shown anything, it is this:

Uncertainty may shape the environment, but it does not define the outcome.

The UAE has already demonstrated its ability to stand steady, be unified across all societies and nationalities and of course, pure resilience.

And it will rise, stronger, sharper, and more united, beyond this moment.

A final thought for leaders during such events

There are moments in leadership where the environment shifts, not dramatically at first, but just enough to unsettle the rhythm of normality and in those moments, what people look for is not perfection, and not even certainty.

They look for **signals**.

Signals in how leaders speak.
How they behave.
How they hold themselves when answers are not yet available.

This reflection is not about events; it is about experience, it is about what happens inside organisations, teams, and individuals when uncertainty moves from the background into the foreground of daily life.

What Became Clear

Uncertainty does not arrive as a single moment; it builds quietly, gradually, until it becomes part of how people think, feel, and operate, and when it does, leadership must shift. Not towards control, but towards **presence**.

Key Leadership Realisations
1. Presence Before Direction

In the early stages, people are not looking for strategy, they are looking for stability, presence, calm, measured, visible, now becomes more powerful than any plan.

2. You Manage People, Not Performance

When attention is divided and clarity is limited, performance becomes a by-product, not the priority.

Focus on:

- Listening
- Observing
- Creating space

Performance will follow.

3. Clarity Over Communication

In uncertain times, more communication is not always better.

What matters is:

- Simplicity
- Consistency
- Relevance

People don't need volume, they need something they can rely on.

4. Fatigue Is Emotional Before It Is Physical

The real impact of uncertainty is not always visible.

It shows in:

- Shortened patience
- Reduced focus
- Quiet withdrawal

Leadership must recognise this early, and adjust accordingly.

5. Consistency Becomes the Strategy

When timelines are unclear and outcomes uncertain, consistency becomes the most reliable form of leadership.

Not intensity.
Not urgency, consistency.

6. Connection Is a Choice

As uncertainty continues, something important happens: people begin to choose connection.

Not because they are told to, but because they need it.

Leaders must create the space for this to happen.

7. Endurance Replaces Reaction

There comes a point where leadership shifts from immediate response to sustained presence.

This is where discipline matters most:

- Showing up the same way
- Holding the same tone
- Providing the same steadiness

Day after day.

What This Means for Leaders

Leadership in uncertainty is not defined by control; it is defined by:

- How you show up
- How you hold others
- How you maintain steadiness when clarity is absent

Because people do not follow certainty, they follow **consistency**.

Final Thought

In the absence of answers, your role as a leader is not to remove uncertainty; it is to ensure that people can continue and that requires one thing above all else:

"Steadiness"

Made in United States
Cleveland, OH
12 May 2026

36515695R10050